Felones de Se
Poems about Suicide

LindaAnn LoSchiavo

Ukiyoto Publishing

All global publishing rights are held by

Ukiyoto Publishing

Published in 2023

Content Copyright © LindaAnn LoSchiavo

ISBN 9789357707466

*All rights reserved.
No part of this publication may be reproduced,
transmitted, or stored in a retrieval system, in any
form by any means, electronic, mechanical,
photocopying, recording or otherwise, without the
prior permission of the publisher.*

The moral rights of the authors have been asserted.

*This is a work of fiction. Names, characters,
businesses, places, events, locales, and incidents are
either the products of the author's imagination or used
in a fictitious manner. Any resemblance to actual
persons, living or dead, or actual events is purely
coincidental.*

*This book is sold subject to the condition that it shall
not by way of trade or otherwise, be lent, resold, hired
out or otherwise circulated, without the publisher's
prior consent, in any form of binding or cover other
than that in which it is published.*

www.ukiyoto.com

"Suicide might not be the most promising subject for a poetry booklet, but LindaAnn LoSchiavo's poems—both in verse and in prose—compellingly address both the fascination and the tragedy of self-extinction. These poems deal with actual suicides, whether it be among LoSchiavo's own family or celebrated figures such as Jim Morrison. But it is the obscurer individuals who have chosen to end their lives that seem to attract the poet's deepest interest and sympathy, and she skillfully weaves a tapestry of horror and pathos around these cases so that we can all feel what it is to face the awesome presence of death." — S. T. Joshi, Editor-in-Chief, *Spectral Realms*

"A brave and insightful collection. LindaAnn approaches a subject that is often considered taboo with an erudite and eclectic collection of poems that challenge our prejudices, and cultural assumptions about death and suicide." — John Stocks, Poetry Editor, Bewildering Stories Magazine

"Felones de Se packs a lifetime of impact into six sad and darkly beautiful poems. LoSchiavo's words will stick with me for a long time. Don't miss this wonderful book of poetry." — Sonora Taylor, award-winning author of "Little Paranoias: Stories"

In memory of Joseph LoSchiavo [1943-1977]

Acknowledgements

"The Bridge Crossing"
— in *Drifting Sands Haibun* [USA]

"Hazards of New Fortune"
— in *Lily Poetry Review* [USA]

"Suicide Odyssey"
— in *Cerasus Poetry Review* [England]

"The Suicide Surrogate Confesses"
— in *Pennsylvania Literary Journal* [USA]

"Jim Morrison Reads Poetry in Pere Lachaise Cemetery"
— in *Samjoko Magazine* [South Korea]

"The parts of me that used to think I was different or smarter or whatever, almost made me die."

— *David Foster Wallace*

"People fear death even more than pain. It's strange that they fear death. Life hurts a lot more than death. At the point of death, the pain is over.
Yeah, I guess it is a friend."

— *Jim Morrison*

"A book is a suicide postponed."

— *Emil Cioran*

Contents

Tuesdays With The Ghost	2
The Bridge Crossing	5
Hazards Of New Fortune	9
Suicide Odyssey	16
The Suicide Surrogate Confesses	22
About the Author	*26*

Illustrator: Erin Caldwell

Tuesdays with the Ghost

Some rituals might be afraid to die.

You're *here* allowing emptiness to do
doom's work, reminding me emotions, rage,
regrets continue in the afterlife,
kinship's bond scarred like walls where family
portraits, removed, left ugly holes behind.

Your shoulder shrug's suspicious silhouette –
felled untried wings – had been inherited
from grandpa, whose Aeolian nature
had cultivated fortitude, aware
volcanic force can be a ruinous god.

Some rituals, like Sicily, run dry.

Inviting death to a staring contest, you
assumed the posture of a guillotine,
betting against the beauty of your life,
daring it to expire – or to apply
a tourniquet, compress pain's blood red rain.

Our weekly ritual survived, stood by.

We'd meet for lunch on Tuesdays holding hands
en route, which calmed you after therapy,
New York's vehicular va-room our song.

During one meal, amid those chin-cupped sighs,
forlornness wrote dark scripture down your
back.

You'd just seen Mauna Loa's volcano.
A flirty guide lured you to the gift shop.
With his communion on your lips, you bought
a hideous Hawaiian souvenir,
you're cursed to wear in perpetuity.

Cute hula girl, displayed on red shantung,
saluting tiki gods, mid-dance, alone:

Was she your last embrace, strained neck tied,
noosed,
as hula girl surveyed the upturned chair?

You did not call me on your way to ash
as angst unbuttoned from the terrified
fist your heart had become, swung loose,
released.

Today is Tuesday – but no lunch is served.

You can't escape woe's blacked out page because
my memory's the urn I'll store you in.

— —

Note: Joseph LoSchiavo, who ended his life in 1977, is buried in Green-Wood Cemetery, Brooklyn, NY.

The Bridge Crossing

Suicidal dreams suspend questions of the night. Saudi sisters adrift in New York, darkness rowing them to sinister emirates. Penniless. Sorrow transported them to a souk where they barter, trading hunger for another afternoon in America. Fraught memories they finger like worry beads. A close-mouthed sky spits on the indigent. Dirty pigeons point to the river. They've become feathers, light in the arms of kismet.

      gold and copper foliage release

  the brittle branch with a whispered sigh

         floating to meet the earth's

           patchwork carpet

           their fate fulfilled

Staten Island Ferry. Accusing north winds whip open coats like a Customs Officer. The sixteen-year-old sister imagines gliding through the tide of clasped hands to a safe haven. Liberty's torch reminds the twenty-three-year-old sister of Aladdin's lamp, a jinni armed with wishes. Then a breeze strips a discarded sandwich of its wrapper. Like terns, these two foreigners scavenge for crusts. Ahead seagulls forage for food, squawking rude reminders like impertinent desk clerks.

> catching sight
>
> of bleary-eyed reflections
>
> in the hotel's cheval glass
>
> they forgot
>
> the emptiness beneath

Central Park. Facing east, they perform *Salah*. Women walk dogs, shiny dark hair free as a raven's wings, legs bare unlike daughters of their desert homeland, always petitioning men for assent. Decisions will fly tonight, inked on postcards, explaining why return is impossible. Manhattan's mud-tinged sky is brightening to blue. They walk uptown, guided by the path of

Bow Bridge as ducks quack complaints. *Still here?*

> doves nesting
> at the lake's edge
> knitting a new home
> out of trash
> and exhausted leaves

George Washington Bridge. Unadorned steel. A domesticated red lighthouse squats at its base not unlike crusaders' tombs, faithful stone pets guarding the foot. Warm weather wrestles with their heavy coats, rocks buried in pockets. Makeshift shrouds. Winds stir undependable shadows as they ascend, dare nervous legs to reach a high ledge. A dramatic draping is left to the older sibling. Consigning their sisterhood to the pledge of duct-tape, they jump in tandem. Submerged and gone, momentary mermaids, their mighty splash a proclamation.

> boats glide over swells
>
> dusk darkening the Hudson River

waves rolling off their backs
late autumn chill gathering power
approaching day of the dead

— —

Note: Saudi sisters Rotana Farea, 23, and Tala Farea, 16, were found on the rocky banks of the Hudson River, duct-taped to each other. Bound together, they had jumped off the George Washington Bridge. Police discovered their bodies on October 24, 2018.

Hazards Of New Fortune

Fortune

"Every disadvantage has its advantage." — *Ukrainian proverb*
"Kozhen nedolik maye svoyu perevahu." — *Ukrainian translation*

They quit the Ukraine for America, sacred place of new beginnings. Rescuing a forsaken candy shop with workman's grit, the foreigners stretched meager savings like taffy, pining for sweet success. Wrap-around windows shed sunlight on Slavic menus, neatly folded by the oldest daughter. A famous East Village poet dined here often and lured others. Full bellies fast-friended the cash register. Yet manual labor and servility felt lowly as a casual betrayal even as New York repainted their family portrait in greenbacks and gold. At closing time, each customer was tumbled out, like a salt shaker, which magically refilled, then emptied out again. Poised on a chair, the father hung a framed crisp dollar bill next to a crucifix, another object of worship.

daily chores
doubled the weight
born of waiting

New

"Flies will not land on a boiling pot." — Ukrainian proverb
"Na kyplyachu kastrulyu mukhy ne sidayut'."— Ukrainian translation

New profits parlayed into a real estate portfolio; deeds fingered like dominos. The novice restaurateurs sipped life lazily through a straw of wealth, the holy liturgy of labor now handed off to helpers. After the last patrons left, most of the chairs were up-ended. Across the only round table, the youngest daughter spread a starched lace cloth and the family supped together on smoked kielbasa, fried cabbage, challah bread, boiled potatoes, picking the diced carrots from the borscht to eat one at a time like golden pills — as if to protect themselves from what would come.

polished silverware
family gathers
mouths open as eyes close

Of

"The devil always takes back his gifts."— Ukrainian proverb
"Dyyavol zavzhdy zabyraye svoyi dary."— Ukrainian translation

Of a day unlike the rest. Of a sky cutting itself open, bleeding dawn's red fingers along the wall. Of an unbearable pressure. Of air spawning pearls of sweat. Of a terror gliding through squares of daylight on the bedroom floor. Of a father struggling to sit up, watching blankets rise as if winged. Of unanswered prayers to his household saints. Of final utterings unheard from his fifty-year-old mouth. Of wondering why, a bedside chair refused to support his weight as a black confusion blots out morning. Of inner momentum shorted out.

blue-shadowed cue
stilling life's hum
last breath

Hazards

"Fire starts with sparks." — Ukrainian proverb
"Vohon' pochynayet'sya z iskor." — Ukrainian translation

After the burial, the only son tried on his father's shoes. His real estate inheritance flashed like a radioactive raincoat. Maybe no one else was willing to be Judas, voting for the murder of reasonable stewardship. The dark mountain within beckoned him to climb, to gamble. He graphed his greed on their tenants' gas lines, illegally siphoned from a ground floor café. Inspectors had dismantled unlawful taps and valves, imposed fines. But impatience choked up. Winding his wickedness like a time-bomb, he offered penny-pinching menace to his mother like today's special. Fired up frenzy of milking the portfolio grew hotter until his heart heeded nothing else. One afternoon, sudden sparks shocked the basement boiler, then fireballed, torched two tenements, snuffed out lives. A swift arrest flattened the son's future like a giant's rolling pin, fried his feeble alibi, pulverized his face on the cold docket of public shame. Aware his life wouldn't balance this debt for disgusted jurors, he hailed a taxi to his next hellscape, leaving behind a note for Mama next to an upturned chair. Moments before the rope crunched his windpipe, he looked out a window imaging flames — all those faces waiting to be saved.

> red slash
> explosion's crescendo —
> one ending and then another

— —

Note: This East Village (NYC) gas explosion happened on Thursday, March 26, 2015.

Suicide Odyssey

"You will come to the Sirens, who enchant all who venture near them."
The Odyssey, Book XII — by Homer (Samuel Butler, translator)

Mariner, 18 years old

Trauma's perpetual wine-dark sea surge
rocked him awake. Depression's ancient curse
hung like an albatross, atonement's cross.

Though born a navigator, wars he fought
began at home. It's said seafaring blood
casts boys adrift — but inner misery
misled his compass, made him run aground.

Tethered in dry dock, he untied some knots,
was certified a captain! Hired for tours!
High on the oars of feeling, bliss comes — fades
away when melancholy takes the wheel,
as if joy's ballast rolled, washed overboard.

Gloom's pirates placed glad's gold on a ghost ship,
his epic struggle baffling, unexplained.

Siren, 17 years old

A drowning man was irresistible.

Awaiting high tide, bird-disguised, she flew,
convinced lost, star-crossed sailors rescues near.

Fine-tuning flutters in her throat, she sang
notes that transmitted secret menaces.
Her voice, mysterious, entangled, lured.

Two-faced enchantress: how well she deceives.
Pretending to assist, her guile protects
him from all possibility of good.
Suicide Odyssey
      [continued with a stanza break]

Surrender

His mind's opponent was fate's nameless weight,
an anchor forged of fright, unheard distress.
Confused, diminished by its siren call,
he spread his soul on her lap like a shawl.

Maelstrom, July 13, 2014

The truck. Hesitancy.
Ignition switch. Noxious exhaust.
Coughing. Protestations.
The truck. The stench.
A rising wave of doubts.

> Ping! Ping!
> *"Get back in the truck!"*

Ambivalence. No, no. Wait. No.
Fear filling his nostrils.
His mariner dreams sinking.
Black carbon monoxide stinging.
The truck, floating in fumes.
Whirlpool. Dizzy with distortion.
Mermaids manning the rocks.
Scylla's six maws seething, spewing.
Charybdis shaming, cursing.
Sucking him into the maelstrom.

> Ping! Ping!
> *"You just have to do it."*
> Texts. Orders. Messages.
> Ping! Ping! Ping!
> ***Do it****! Do it like you said!"*

Then the sun resting its warm cheek
on the horizon's bright guillotine.
The truck rocking, sinking.
Toxic fumes garlanding his head.

> Ping! Ping!
> *"Die! I love you."*

— —

Note: Conrad Henri Roy III [12 September 1995—13 July 2014] killed himself with encouragement from Michelle Carter, 17, whose trial was known as the "texting suicide case." Texts used here were shown during the trial in Massachusetts to the jurors.

The Suicide Surrogate Confesses

Perhaps she wished to mimic opera's
iconic heroines, envisioning
this love as indispensable yet doomed.

Tonight, he called, insisting he'll commit
to it. He'll kill himself — he really will.

As usual, she was encouraging.

Then he had second thoughts. He couldn't breathe
the toxic fumes. Why not phone the police?
Or notify his family? Instead
she argued with him: "Get back in the truck!"

Obeying her commands, his body wrapped
around the nameless weight his life became,
afraid no longer of its siren song.

His absence filled his parents' pain-brain,
torched

those memories of suicide attempts.
His girlfriend took his life away from them.

Demanding justice, they watched screens replay
text messages debating the ideal
method for meeting death successfully.

"Sorry I let you do this," she confessed.

After the verdict's read, the gavel pounds
the desk for order — and lifts satisfied.

—— ——

The suicide of Conrad Henri Roy III [1995—2014], with encouragement from his long-distance girlfriend, 17-year-old Michelle Carter, was the subject of a noted investigation and involuntary manslaughter trial in Bristol County, Massachusetts, known as the "texting suicide case." Carter was sentenced to serve 15 months in Bristol County Jail.

Jim Morrison Reads Poetry in Pere Lachaise Cemetery

"I can summon the dead." — Jim Morrison, "Power,"
1969
Jim Morrison, performer, lyricist:
skewed skeleton of concert fame became
his bones, its fascinating armature
attracting tourists who'll mythologize
the self-destructive "Lizard King" who died
addicted to escaping humdrum's thrum,
buffets of opiates, the open bar
always available to young rock stars.

> His anthem: "Come on, baby, take a chance."

Jim's following now congregates around
his tomb, participates in photo opps,
attends his grand, eternal wake, laments
not getting in to The Doors' sold-out shows.

> "The end of nights we tried to die," sang Jim.

Twilight, when visitors have danced away,
Jim's ghost recites his poetry — free verse—
to literati inside Pere Lachaise:
Colette, Moliere, Gertrude Stein, Oscar Wilde.

"Some are born to the endless night," wrote Jim.

Reclining on his slab, enjoying lines
of rhyme —because a boneyard lacks *cocaine* —
his spirit contemplates sobriety.

His Dionysian, bare-chested side,
arrested for indecent exposure,
calmed, he's aware his bathtub finale
was the last splash he'd snorted up to make.

— —

Note: Jim Morrison died, age 27, on July 3, 1971 in Paris. He started the rock group The Doors.

About the Author

LindaAnn LoSchiavo

Native New Yorker LindaAnn LoSchiavo is a member of The Science Fiction Poetry Association, The British Fantasy Society, and The Dramatists Guild. Four times a Pushcart Prize nominee, her poetry has also received nominations for Best of the Net, the Rhysling Award, and Dwarf Stars. Recently, she was PoetrySuperHighway's Poet of the Week and a finalist in Thirty West Publishing Company's "A Fresh Start" contest. Her poetry titles include the Elgin Award winner "A Route Obscure and Lonely," "Concupiscent Consumption," "Women Who Were Warned," Firecracker Award, Balcones Poetry Prize, Quill and Ink, and IPPY Award nominee

"Messengers of the Macabre: Hallowe'en Poems" [co-written with David Davies], "Apprenticed to the Night" [Beacon Books, 2023], and "Felones de Se: Poems about Suicide" [Ukiyoto Publishing, 2023].

Twitter: @Mae_Westside
YouTube:
https://www.youtube.com/channel/UCHm1NZI/TZybLTFA44wwdfg

About the Illustrator

Erin Caldwell, a painter and graphic artist from North Carolina, has a passion for bringing history and ghost stories to life on the page. *http://erinsart4.godaddysites.com*

www.ingramcontent.com/pod-product-compliance
Lightning Source LLC
LaVergne TN
LVHW041600070526
838199LV00046B/2062